Buoy

HOME AT SEA

BRUCE BALAN

ILLUSTRATIONS BY

Raúl Colón

浮　標

浮標、海鷗與海豹的生命對話

文字　布魯斯貝倫

插畫　洛爾科隆

翻譯　晨星編譯組

晨星出版

Contents
目　次

來自海洋

　　浮標，不過是一具設置在海上的航行警告標誌，它遠離海岸、處境孤單。站在岸上，我們不難想像它那孤單、寂寥的海上生活。

　　浮標被賦與了生命、賦與了心情及感覺，這座永遠浮在海面不倒翁似的浮標，無論白天晚上，無論風平浪靜或是暴風雨，它引以自豪地認真工作。它隨浪浮蕩、響著鈴鐺聲、閃爍出紅燈警示，不止如此，它遇到船隻、遇到巨鯨、海豚、鯊魚、螃蟹等，浮標和他們朋友般的招呼講話；它的生命裡有晨曦、有夕陽、有星星陪它聊天；它被海豹當作日曬陽台、被海鷗當作是棲身處所……

　　浮標，出我們意料之外的，它活得豐富又多采。

　　是海洋無窮的驚奇和無止盡的曠闊給予浮標鮮活的生命。

　　海風將隨您翻閱浮標的每一頁；您將會在字裡行間聞到海洋飄逸的氣味。

　　透過優美的繪圖及簡明的小故事，本書將帶領我們的腳程踏入海洋，讓我們的視線看到海洋，也提醒我們思索到，一個微不足道的小生命如何在一個豐美開闊的領域中重要起來。

　　浮標一點也不在意，它喜愛海，而且它時常說，這裡是我們的家。

廖鴻基　1998.11

buoy

Buoy rolled lazily on the long low swell of the Sea. Buoy lived far from land; so far that only on the days when the Clouds raced against each other and the Wind seemed a bit angry, could Buoy just barely, ever so slightly, make out something to the east that was neither the Sea nor the Sky. But Buoy didn't mind at all. He loved the Sea and the Sky. He loved their blueness and wondered how it could be that his redness complemented them so perfectly.

浮 標

　　海潮舒緩低平，浮標在上面慵懶地滾動。浮標的位置離陸地好遙，好遠，只有在諸雲相爭，海風微怒的日子，浮標才能稍稍勉強地辨別出東邊那一塊非屬海和天之物，但是浮標一點也不在意。他愛海愛天，他愛海天的藍，他也驚訝，自己的紅竟然能跟海天的藍相襯地如此完美無缺！

Buoy had a bell. He thought that a bell was probably the most delightful thing to have in all the world. On warm, calm nights when the Wind had gone to bed early and every Star that ever was had come out to hear him, he would ring slowly and softly so that his music would have a chance to linger awhile by the Sea before beginning its journey to Heaven. And on cold foggy mornings, when the air was almost too sleepy to carry any noise at all, he would ring as boldly and solidly as he could, so that boats would have no question as to who he was and where he lived. And in times of the gravest danger, when the Wind went screaming in search of its past, and ships lost their way and wandered from the safe path to the west, he would ring loudly and urgently, to warn of the disaster that would occur if his call was not heeded.

浮標有個鈴鐺。他認為，擁有鈴鐺大概是世界上最愉快的事了。在溫暖沉靜的夜，風兒早早入睡，而所有星星都探頭出來時，他就會緩緩地，輕輕地搖，讓樂音在出發往天堂旅行之前，有機會在海上稍加停留。寒冷的早晨大霧迷漫，空氣還太睏倦，承載不了一丁點聲音時，他會盡量勇敢、堅決地搖，讓行船能毫無疑慮地知道他是誰，還有他所在的位置。在最危險的時刻，狂風嚎嘯，行船迷失方向，往西漂泊偏離安全的航道時，他就會搖出巨大、急迫的聲音警告說，若不聽他的呼喚，就會有災難降臨。

Buoy also had a light. It sat on the top of his head. It was a red light, and Buoy could flash it. At first it had been very hard to remember how to do it just rihgt. But now, Buoy had been doing it for so long that he didn´t even have to think about it.

　浮標也有一盞燈。那盞燈坐在他的頭頂。燈是紅色的，而且浮標可以讓它一眨一眨地閃。起初，很難學會怎麼閃得恰恰好。但現在，浮標操作久了，連想都不用去想就能很順了。

Flash flash flash; wait...wait...wait...wait.

Flash flash flash; wait...wait...wait...wait.

...Flash flash flash.

Buoy never missed a flash or waited too long. And on the blackest of nights, when the Moon was visiting relatives far away, Buoy would concentrate as hard as he could to force his light through the darkness so that ships and boats would know that he was there to keep them on the safe path.

Buoy lived very far from land where people think it is lonely.

But for Buoy, it was home.

閃閃閃；等……等……等……等。

閃閃閃……；等……等……等。

……閃閃閃。

浮標沒有錯失過任何一次閃光，也不會遲疑太久。最深的暗夜裡，當月亮遠行探訪親友，浮標就會盡可能集中精神放出光芒，穿透黑暗，讓行走中的大小船隻知道他在那裡，以確保他們留在安全的水道上。

浮標的住處離陸地如此遙遠，人們以爲他孤處一方。

但對浮標而言，那裡就是他的家。

ship

Buoy could hear the ship coming when it was still a long way off.

Gull slept with his head under his wing.

Seal lay on her back. She liked the way the sunlight bounced on her belly.

"Ship coming," said Buoy.

No one moved.

"Ship coming," said Buoy again, and he rang his bell.

"Oh," said Seal

"So...?" said Gull.

"Don´t you care?" asked Buoy.

"No," said Seal.

"You´ve seen one ship, you´ve seen´em all," said Gull. "A ship´s not like a hurricane or a herring, you know." He and Seal closed their eyes.

船

　　船還在遙遠的彼方時，浮標就聽見了。

　　海鷗將頭藏在翅膀下熟睡著。

　　海豹仰臥海面，她喜歡陽光在肚皮上跳躍的感覺。

　　「船來了。」浮標說。

　　大家都動也不動。

　　「船來了。」浮標又叫了一次，而且搖一搖鈴鐺。

　　「嗯。」海豹說。

　　「是嗎……？」海鷗說。

　　「你們不在乎嗎？」浮標問。

　　「不在乎。」海豹說。

　　「船都一樣嘛，見過一艘，就等於見過全部了。」海鷗說：「船不像颶風，也不像鯡魚，你是知道的。」他和海豹閉起了眼睛。

Buoy didn´t say anything. He knew they wouldn´t understand. He loved ships. A Ship-Coming was what he lived for. A Ship-Coming was *important*. He knew this the way he knew the sound of his bell. He knew, and he waited.

Slowly it approached from the north, its hugeness so small when it was far away. This one was a freighter; or so Buoy guessed, based on what Gull had once told him.

Closer and closer. Larger and larger. The ship seemed to grow out of the Sea. Buoy felt its thrumming deep inside his belly. He rolled with the swell. He flashed his light and rang his bell.

"Stay to the west," he whispered. "Stay to the west."

And the ship responded as if it heard. It altered course, leaving Buoy to port. But only by a few hundred feet.

浮標什麼也沒說。他知道，他們不會瞭解。他愛船。行駛過來的船是他生命的寄託；行駛過來的船很重要。他知道這一點就像他知道自己的鈴鐺聲一樣。他確定，也不停地等待。

　　慢慢的，它從北而來，它的巨大在遠方顯得極為渺小，這一艘是貨輪，浮標這樣子猜想著，照著海鷗教他的方式。

　　愈來愈近，愈來愈大了。這艘船彷彿從海裡長出來似的，浮標感覺到肚子裡震動的聲音。他隨著潮水滾動，閃出亮光，搖響鈴聲。

　　「保持西向，」他輕聲說，「保持西向。」

　　船保持西向，好像聽到了他的話。它改變航道，避開浮標，駛向港口。但僅僅距離幾百呎而已。

Buoy looked up at the massive wall that slid past. He had kept it to the west. He had kept it safe from harm.

As the ship passed, its huge wake raced toward Buoy. He braced himself. He thought of warning Gull and Seal, but they had said they didn't want to be disturbed.

浮標抬頭看見如牆的巨大船身滑過，他順利地讓船隻駛向西方，留在安全的航道，不受傷害。

當船身駛過，巨大的浪頭衝向浮標。他做好準備。他想到要警告海鷗與海豹，可是，他們說過，他們不要被打擾。

The wake hit with a splash. Buoy rocked noisily, throwing Seal into the Sea and knocking Gull off his perch.

They spluttered and grumbled as they made their way back to their resting spots.

"Thanks for the warning, Buoy," Gull muttered.

"My pleasure," answered Buoy, still smiling because he had done his job. He had done it well.

航跡激濺起水花，浮標嘩啦嘩啦地搖晃出吵鬧聲，把海豹拋入海中，而海鷗也被搖得脫離棲身之處，他們嘟嘟嚷嚷地爬回原來休息的地點。

　　「多謝你的警告，浮標。」海鷗喃喃說著。

　　「我的榮幸，」浮標回答，依然面帶微笑，因為他已盡到職責，而且表現出色。

whale song

Porpoise was visiting. She looked toward the horizon. "I hear Whales," she said.

Porpoise was swimming next to Seal while Gull, as usual, stood on Buoy's head, leaning into the Wind.

"Are they close?" asked Buoy hopefully.

"Very," said Porpoise.

Everyone listened.

"I don't hear anything," said Gull.

"Shhh," said Seal

Everyone listened.

"I still don't hear anything," said Gull grumpily.

鯨魚之歌

　　海豚來訪。她看著海平面，「我聽到鯨魚。」她說。

　　海豚伴著海豹游泳，而海鷗和平常一般，站在浮標的頭上，迎著風。

　　「他們在附近嗎？」浮標語帶期盼問道。

　　「很近。」海豚說。

　　大家都注意聽。

　　「我沒聽見什麼聲音。」海鷗說。

　　「噓。」海豹說。

　　大家都注意聽。

　　「我還是什麼都沒有聽見。」海鷗不高興地說。

"Shhh!" said Seal again.

Everyone listened. Gull shifted from one foot to the other.

"I hear them," whispered Seal.

Buoy listened hard. Faint tones swam through the blue Sea. Buoy heard the Whale song. It sounded very much like the song the Stars sang on crystal nights. But not so clear. And not so distant.

No one spoke. Except Gull, who harrumphed every few minutes.

They all listened.

It was a very old song. Though they could not understand it—Porpoise could pick out a few phrases here and there—they knew it was old. Older than Shark. Older than Rain. Even older than the Sea. Porpoise said it told of the first day of the Sea. And how the first Whale swam on that first day. And how the first Whale sang. And how the song created itself and everything else as

「噓！」海豹又說。

大家注意聽，海鷗換腳站立。

「我聽到了。」海豹小聲說。

浮標仔細地聽。隱隱約約的聲音游過碧藍的大海。浮標聽見了鯨魚的歌，聽起來很像是星星在晶亮的夜唱歌，只是沒有那麼清楚，也不那麼遙遠。

誰都不說話，除了海鷗，海鷗每隔幾分鐘就嘎叫一聲。

他們全都傾聽著。

那是很老的一首歌。雖然他們聽不懂——海豚有時可以聽懂其中幾個字——他們知道那首歌的年代古老，比鯊魚更古老；比雨水更古老；甚至於比大海更古老。海豚說鯨魚之歌敘述著大海創始的那一天，以及第一條鯨魚如何在初始的那天游泳，還有第一條鯨魚如何歌唱、那首歌如何創

27

well. There was much more, but it was too ancient for any of them ever to grasp.

The singing grew louder. Gray shapes appeared in the blue distance.

"I see them!" cried Buoy.

Closer they came. Moving the water with their magnificence. The sweep of their great flukes a metronome to their song.

When they were finally very close, Buoy spoke.

"Hello, Whales!" he called.

"Hello, Buoy," said one.

"Who do you sing to?" asked Buoy.

"We sing to the Stars," said the Whale.

"Why?"

"To let them know that we are here, and that we are watching still."

造自己和其他的一切。另外還有許多故事，但是歌曲實在太古老了，他們之中沒有任何人能捕捉到它的眞意。

歌聲愈來愈響亮，灰色的形體在遙遠深邃的碧藍中逐漸顯現。

「我看見他們了！」浮標叫道。

他們更靠近了。雄偉的軀體逐水而來，巨大的尾翼橫掃著，像是歌聲的節拍器。

當他們終於靠近過來時，浮標開口了。

「哈囉，鯨魚！」他喊道。

「哈囉，浮標。」一隻鯨魚說。

「你們在對誰歌唱？」浮標問道。

「我們在對星星歌唱。」鯨魚說。

「爲什麼？」

「告訴他們，我們在這裡，而且仍然凝視著。」

"What are you watching?" asked Buoy.

But the Whale had slid past, the dark blue closing behind him as he went.

　「你們在看什麼？」浮標問。

　可是鯨魚已滑過身去，暗藍的海水在其身後
收攏起來。

Flowing like the great ocean currents, the Whales had little time to stay and talk.

When their shapes had faded into the distance, and the last note of their song had quietly passed by on its long journey, Gull spoke.

"Can I talk now?" he said, still cranky.

"No," Buoy said gently.

And they all floated in silence, remembering.

隨著海潮漂游，這群鯨魚沒有時間逗留，也沒有時間說話。

　　當他們的身影逐漸淡入遠方，歌聲的最後一個音符，在其悠長的旅途靜靜消散時，海鷗開口了。

　　「我現在可以說話了嗎？」他說，仍在鬧彆扭。

　　「不可以。」浮標溫柔地應道。

　　他們全都在沉默之中漂浮並記憶著。

sailboat

Buoy let the Wind rock him gently. It was the laziest of days. The Sun was hot, and it made him sleepy. So sleepy that he didn´t notice the small sailboat until it was quite close. There was no swell running; the Sea was thinking and couldn´t be bothered to make waves today. Only the Breeze, which was very quiet so as not to disturb the Sea, wrinkled the smooth blueness a bit. The sailboat came slowly; white sails and deep green hull. It leaned over just a little with the light Wind. Several big people sat in the back. A small person sat in the front. His legs dangled over the edge and occasionally touched the water in a line of white bubbles. He sat leaning with his arms against the lifelines and looked out hard.

帆 船

　　浮標讓風輕輕搖著他。那是最慵懶的日子，陽光熾熱，使他昏昏欲睡，他睏極了，差點忽略了一艘已經相當靠近的小帆船。沒有奔騰的潮湧，今天海在思考，懶得興起波浪。只有微風，沉靜非常，不願驚動海，只把那平滑的藍吹起些許波紋。帆船來勢輕緩，雪白的帆布，深綠的船身。在微風中，它只微微傾斜，幾個大塊頭坐在後面，一個小個子坐在前頭。他的雙腳懸在船沿，有時候會碰到海水，畫出白色的泡沫線條。他斜坐著，雙臂吊著救生索，目光緊盯著海面。

Buoy thought the small one was looking at him. The boat sailed closer. Buoy was sure the boy was looking right at him. Splashes came from the place where the bow kissed the Sea. The boat moved as if it were coasting down a long gentle hill.

The boy stared at Buoy. And just as the boat passed—so close that Buoy could have touched it if he had leaned over a little—the small one said gently, "Hello, Buoy." This, so quietly that Buoy wasn´t even sure he had heard it. He was amazed. No person had ever spoken to him. They would often wave and bark at Seal, and either curse or screech at Gull, but they never spoke to Buoy.

浮標心想，這小個子在注視他。船愈來愈靠近，浮標確定，這男孩正直視著他。船首觸及海面，興起水花，船彷彿沿著一座長而平緩的小山往前行進。

　　男孩盯著浮標。當船身經過時──船離得好近，彷彿浮標再多傾斜那麼一點點，就可以摸到船身──小個子溫柔地說：「哈囉，浮標。」聲音極為輕緩，浮標甚至不能相信自己聽到了。他好驚訝，因為從來沒有人跟他說過話。他們常會對著海豹揮手、大叫，或是對著海鷗咒罵、尖叫，可是，他們從不跟浮標說話。

By the time Buoy had recovered himself, the boat and the boy had sailed a good way off. Buoy rang his bell twice. And then a third time. He thought he saw the boy turn back...and wave.

　　浮標回神過來時，帆船和男孩已經走遠了。浮標搖了兩次鈴，接著再搖第三次，他覺得他看見男孩轉過身來......向他揮了揮手。

green flash

Sometimes—not always, just sometimes—when the Sea was calm and the air was clear and the horizon was so crisp and sharp and straight that Seal and Gull and Buoy were almost absolutely certain that the world was flat; sometimes, at sunset, they would wait for the Green Flash.

Seal would sit up eagerly while Gull stood intently atop Buoy. All would stare into the sunset, waiting for the top edge of the great orange ball to disappear below the horizon. For at that moment, sometimes, when everything was just right, the Sky would, for just half a second, glow green. And then it would be night.

綠光

　　有時候──並非一直，只是有時候──大海寧靜，空氣清爽，海平線明晰、筆直，使海豹、海鷗和浮標都幾乎確信地球是平坦的；有時候，夕陽西下時，他們會等待綠光的來臨。

　　海豹會急切地坐起來，海鷗則專心地站在浮標頭上。他們全都凝視著夕陽，等待橘色大圓球頂端消失在海平線，因為在那一剎那，有時候一切都恰到時機，天空就會變成綠色，只維持短暫的半秒鐘，緊接著，就夜幕低垂了。

Gull said it was a signal from the Sun to the Stars, telling them that it was time to come out. But Seal said it was when the Sun went down too close to the Sea and its yellow flames brushed against the Sea´s blue waves. Gull said that was ridiculous and Seal said that it wasn´t.

海鷗說，那是太陽發給星星的訊號，告訴他們該出來了。但海豹說，那是因為太陽落下去時太靠近海，它的黃色火焰掠過海的藍色波浪所擦出的效果。海鷗說，那太荒謬了，海豹回嘴道，才不會呢！

And occasionally Porpoise would come by and say that they were both wrong and that she knew what the Green Flash was but wasn't going to tell.

Buoy thought he might know. He had a hazy idea that there was another Buoy far away flashing in the night, and sometimes, with the help of the Sun, its light shone all the way across the Sea so that Buoy would know he wasn't alone. He never told Gull and Seal about this, but once he told Porpoise and she said that it wasn't very far from the truth. Buoy asked how far and where Truth was anyway. Was it to the west? The north? Porpoise smiled and said it didn't really matter.

But Buoy thought it did. So, whenever the time was right for the Green Flash, he flashed his own light. He flashed it as brightly as he could, hoping the other Buoy would see. Hoping the other Buoy would know he wasn't alone either.

有時，海豚會靠過來。她說，他們兩個都錯了。她知道綠光的成因，卻不肯透露。

　　浮標認為自己可能知道，他隱約知曉遠方另外有一個浮標在晚上閃著光，有些時候，藉著太陽的幫助，那道閃光會越過海洋，讓浮標知道他並不孤單。他從沒告訴海鷗和海豹這個想法，可是，他告訴過海豚一次，而海豚回答，浮標說的與事實相差不遠。浮標就問她，到底離事實有多遠。它在西方嗎？還是北方？海豚只一逕地微笑，她說，那並不重要。

　　可是浮標覺得那是重要的事。所以不論何時，只要時機適合綠光，他就會閃出他的光。他盡可能閃得又明又亮，期待那一個浮標能夠看見。他希望另外那個浮標知道，他也不孤單。

shark

Slowly he swam by. Not very often and not very fast. Dark in the blue water. He didn´t like to talk. And he never spoke first.

"Hello, Shark," Buoy would say.

There would, of course, be no answer. "Hello, Shark," he´d say again. Then he´d wait some more as Shark circled and circled.

But, as always on the second try, no reply.

And when he could wait no longer, Buoy would clang his bell and shout, "*Hello, Shark*!"

When he finally spoke, Shark´s voice was quiet, not cold. Mellow, not mean. And very, very patient.

鯊 魚

慢慢地，他游了過來。他不常來，速度也不
很快。在藍色的海水中顯得黝黑。他不喜歡說
話，也從不先開口。

「哈囉，鯊魚。」浮標會這樣說。

當然，沒有回應。

「哈囉，鯊魚。」他又說了一次。鯊魚繞了又
繞，浮標繼續等待。

但是，總是這樣子的，第二次開口，仍然沒
有回答。

當浮標沒辦法再等待時，他會用力搖鈴，大
叫：「哈囉，鯊魚！」

鯊魚終於開口了。他的聲音冷靜而不冷漠，
柔和而不凶惡，而且顯得極有耐心。

"hello," Shark said, "hello, buoy. How is life?"

"It´s wonderful!" answered Buoy. "And how is life for you?"

"hungry," Shark said. "hungry, and long."

「哈囉，」鯊魚說：「哈囉，浮標，日子過得如何？」

「棒極了！」浮標回答說：「你的日子過得怎麼樣？」

「饑餓，」鯊魚說：「饑餓，餓好久了。」

Seal looked warily over Buoy's edge, down into the water at Shark circling around and around.

"There's no food here, Shark," said Seal. "Maybe you should look somewhere else."

"maybe," said Shark, slowly circling still. "maybe..."

Seal moved a little farther from the edge. She was not fond of Shark.

"You wouldn't hurt Seal, would you, Shark?" asked Buoy.

Shark slowed down just a little. There was a long pause. "i am as i was made," he said at last Then he was silent again.

Buoy thought about this. He wasn't quite sure what it meant. Seal, however, was. She moved farther from the edge and closer to Buoy's bell.

海豹從浮標的邊緣憂心地往外探頭，看著鯊魚在水中一圈又一圈地繞。

　　「這裡沒有東西吃啦，鯊魚，」海豹說：「也許你該到別處去找。」

　　「大概吧，」鯊魚說，仍在慢慢兜圈子。「大概吧……」

　　海豹稍稍退離了邊緣，她不喜歡鯊魚。

　　「你不會傷害海豹吧，鯊魚？」浮標說。

　　鯊魚只慢下來一點點。他沈默了好一陣子。「我天生就是這個樣子。」他終於開口，然後又安靜下來。

　　浮標思索著這句話，他不是很懂那句話的意思。可是，海豹懂，她退得離邊緣更遠了，比較靠近浮標的鈴鐺。

Finally, after too long a time for Seal, and too short a time for Shark, Shark swam off—silent and mellow, slow and calm.

"Good-bye, Shark," Buoy said.

Shark never ever said good-bye.

終於，經過對海豹而言太久而對鯊魚來說太短的一段時間，鯊魚游走了，安靜而柔和、緩慢而沉著。

　　「再見，鯊魚。」浮標說。

　　鯊魚從不說再見。

stars

Night came like a blanket of silence spread over the Sea. And woven through the blanket, Buoy´s light—flashing, flashing into the black. Ships in the distance knew exactly where they were when they saw that flash. Ships at night were only lights far away—red or green, and white.

But some nights there were no ships, and Buoy and Gull and Seal and the Sea were left to themselves. Except for the Moon and the Stars.

The Moon, always changing, looked down with clear brightness, and Buoy felt its light deep in his heart. Then, in the silence, Buoy would wait for the Falling Stars.

星 星

　　夜晚像一張無聲的毯子覆蓋著大海。而浮標
的閃光交織在那張毯子上，閃爍著，閃入黑暗
中。船隻遠遠地看到亮光，就知道自己確實的所
在。晚間的船只是遠方的光──有的紅，有的綠，
有的白。

　　有些晚上沒有船，那麼，除了月亮和星星之
外，就只有浮標、海鷗、海豹和海了。

　　月亮一直都在變，帶著清晰皎亮的光芒往下
望，浮標的內心深處能感受其光。然後在寂靜
中，浮標會等待流星的出現。

He'd stare for hours into the black Sky. Sometimes there would be only one or two, or, on the unhappy nights, none. But sometimes there would be dozens. And as each Star raced across the Sky, Buoy could almost feel himself lifted a little out of the Sea, as if the Stars wanted him to follow.

"Where do they land?" asked Buoy.

"They don't land," said Gull authoritatively. "They miss the earth and keep going forever."

"No they don't," said Seal. "They fall on the other edge of the Sea. They make the water warm there. So warm that fish have to jump into the air to cool off."

"That's ridiculous!" said Gull. "Fish wouldn't do that even if the water *was* warm."

他會凝視黑暗的天空好幾個小時。有時候，只會有一顆或二顆；有些不愉快的夜晚，一顆也沒有；但有時候會有好幾十顆。看著流星劃過天際，浮標覺得自己幾乎要飛離海面，彷彿流星要他跟隨一般。

　　「他們會在哪裡降落呢？」浮標問。

　　「他們不在陸地上降落，」海鷗信誓旦旦地說：「他們會經過地球，永遠不斷地走下去。」

　　「不，才不呢，」海豹說：「他們降落在海的另一邊，使那裡的海水熱起來，因為水很熱，魚兒只好跳到空中乘涼。」

　　「太荒謬了！」海鷗說：「水就是熱了，魚也不會那樣子。」

"What makes you so sure?" asked Seal. "You´ve never been there."

"Neither have you. But I could fly there if I wanted."

"Well, I could swim there. And I´d get there first."

「你怎麼那麼有把握？」海豹問：「你又沒去過那裡。」

「你也沒去過呀！但是，如果我願意，我可以飛過去。」

「那我也可以游過去啊！而且，我還會先到呢。」

"Oh yeah?"

"Yeah."

Back and forth they went. Until Seal was barking and Gull was screeching and neither was listening to what the other one was saying at all.

Clang! Clang! Clang!

Buoy rang his bell as loudly as he could. Startled, Gull and Seal stopped bickering. They looked at Buoy.

"Could we just watch the Stars for a while?" he said.

And then added, "Quietly."

And they did.

「是嗎？」

「當然。」

他們你來我往地爭論，直到海豹開始吠叫，海鷗也尖嘯不已，雙方都不再注意聽對方在說些什麼。

噹啷！噹啷！噹啷！

浮標極力搖響鈴噹。海鷗和海豹嚇了一跳，這才停止吵鬧，看著浮標。

「我們可不可以就看著星星？」他說。

接著，他補上一句：「安安靜靜地看。」

他們照做了。

below

Buoy stayed in one spot on the Sea. Because below him, he had a tail of chain that stretched down and down and down and down. Seal could not swim that far down. Nor could Porpoise. Shark didn´t even respond when Buoy asked him to try.

But Buoy knew that his chain went all the way to the floor of the Sea. And though he couldn´t quite explain how he did it, he could sometimes follow the chain all the way down.

This usually happened when he was drifting off for a nap. On hot days, with the waves rolling him gently and no ships in sight, he would sometimes begin to feel drowsy. Back and forth he´d rock. And as he sank into sleep, his spirit would settle, slowly, beneath the waves. And there, he would see...

底下

　　浮標停駐在海上的一個定點。因為，他的底部有一條鏈子，長長地向下延伸再延伸。是那麼地深遠，海豹游不下去，海豚也不行。至於鯊魚，浮標請他幫忙時，他連吭都不吭一聲。

　　但浮標知道，他的長鏈一直向下延伸到海底。有時候他可以隨著鏈子一直沉到海底，雖然他無法解釋清楚自己是怎麼做到的。

　　這通常是他迷迷糊糊打著瞌睡時發生的。在大熱天裡，海浪輕柔地搖著他，沒有任何船隻的蹤影，他有時就會覺得昏昏欲睡，於是前前後後地晃動。當他沉睡時，他的精神會慢慢沉到海浪底下。在那裡，他會看見……

The sea grass hanging below him, swaying back and forth as if forever beckoning to the schools of tiny fish that swam past. The sunlight creating a sparkling roof of illuminated waves above.

海草懸在他底下，擺來擺去，好像永遠在對游過的一群群小魚揮手致意。陽光在明亮的波浪上頭營造出閃耀的屋頂。

Then down the chain. To where the water grew cold. And much larger fish swam by. And Shark ate them. There was no yellow here. No orange. No red.

Then down the chain. To where the light became dim. And green could not dive this deep. Only very dark blue.

Then down the chain. To where there was no color at all. But strange creatures lived here. Creatures that glowed in the darkness.

Then down the chain. To the seabed. And there, rooted in the depth of the Sea, Buoy felt a humming. A hum that seemed to come from deeper than the Sea. It reminded him somehow of the song of the Whales. But he did not hear this song. He felt it. It seemed to be part of who he was. He did not understand that it was *he* who was a part of the *song*.

沿著鏈子下去，來到水較冷的地方，那裡有比較大的魚游過，他們是鯊魚的食糧。那裡沒有黃色，沒有橘色，沒有紅色。

　　沿著鍊子再往下，光線昏暗，綠色也無法深潛在此，只有很深很深的藍。

　　沿著鏈子再往下，就完全沒有顏色了。但是那裡住著奇異的生物，他們在黑暗中發亮。

　　沿著鏈子再往下，到了海床。在那裡，它根植在深海裡。浮標感覺到嗡嗡的聲音，似乎來自比海更深的地方，使他隱約想起鯨魚之歌。但是，他並沒有聽到這首歌，而是用心感受到。那首歌好像是他的一部分。他並不知道，他自己才是那首歌的一部分。

concert

Buoy spun slowly—around and around—scanning the horizon.

No Whales.

"I wish I could sing," he muttered.

No one said anything.

"I wish I could sing," he said again, and then added, "like the Whales."

Gull rolled his eyes, shook his head, and was about to say something when Seal interrupted.

"You sing in your own way, Buoy," she said. "You have your bell."

協奏曲

　　浮標緩緩地旋轉，一轉再轉，檢視著海平線。

　　沒有鯨。

　　「但願我能歌唱。」他嘟嚷著。

　　沒有人答腔。

　　「但願我能歌唱，」他又說了一次，並加了一句：「就像鯨魚那樣。」

　　海鷗轉了轉眼珠子，搖搖頭，正要開口時，海豹插嘴了。

　　「你用自己的方式唱呀，浮標，」她說：「你有鈴鐺呀！」

The thought didn´t cheer Buoy. He loved his bell. He loved the fine clear note it made. But it was only *one* note. And *he* was the only one who played it.

"It´s not the same," he replied sullenly. "The Whales sing together. But there are no other Buoys to play with me."

"We´ll help," Seal offered.

"Who´s we?" Gull asked.

Buoy brightened. "Really?"

"Yes." Seal sat up. "I´ll show you. Ring your bell every time I tap my flipper."

Seal began tapping, and Buoy tried to follow the rhythm.

Clang, cla-clang...Clang, clang.
Clang, cla-clang...Clang, clang.

這個想法沒有讓浮標打起精神。他愛他的鈴鐺，他愛那鈴鐺發出來的雅緻清晰的音符。可是，它只有一個音，而且，只有他在演奏那個音。

　　「那不一樣，」他悶悶不樂地答道：「鯨魚是成群齊唱，可是，沒有別的浮標和我一同演奏。」

　　「我們會幫你。」海豹出點子。

　　「誰是我們？」海鷗問。

　　浮標高興起來。「真的？」

　　「是真的，」海豹坐起身子。「我做給你看，每一次我拍打前肢你就搖鈴。」

　　海豹開始拍打，浮標努力跟著節奏搖鈴。

　　「噹，噹噹……噹，噹。」

　　「噹，噹噹……噹，噹。」

Then Seal turned to Gull. "You give a flap and a screech to the beat of my tail."

"I'm not having any part of this—" Gull began.

"Start *now*," Seal said with a severe look.

Flap-screech, flap-screech...flap-screech, flap-screech.

Seal continued tapping and began adding a few barks of her own.

They practiced all afternoon. At first their song sounded awful, but slowly they improved. Buoy learned to keep the rhythm all by himself. Seal produced different notes by drumming on various parts of Buoy's body. Gull forgot that he wasn't having a good time.

後來，海豹轉向海鷗：「你跟著我尾巴的節拍鼓動翅膀，同時尖叫一聲。」

　　「我才不要加入這⋯⋯。」海鷗說。

　　「現在開始。」海豹神情嚴肅地說。

　　「鼓翅—尖叫，鼓翅—尖叫⋯⋯鼓翅—尖叫，鼓翅—尖叫。」

　　海豹繼續打拍子，同時開始加上自己的幾聲吠叫。

　　他們練習了整個下午。起初他們的歌聲真難聽，但慢慢的，他們有了進步。浮標學著只靠自己穩住節奏。海豹敲打著浮標身體的各個部位，製造出不同的樂音。海鷗則忘了他剛剛的不愉快。

The Sun sank low. Still they played on. The Stars came out to listen, but the musicians didn´t notice. Each was lost in the music they were creating together.

Finally, knowing deep down that it was just the right moment.

太陽慢慢下沉了，他們卻還在演奏。星星探頭傾聽，但是這些音樂家並沒有發覺，他們每一個都陶醉在共同創造的音樂聲中。

最後，他們發自內心地感覺到那是最美好的時刻。

They ended their song with a magnificent finale of barks, screeches, and clangs.

Silence.

And then...splashes, whistles, and hoots!

The three musicians opened their eyes. An audience had gathered. Porpoise was there, as well as several sea lions, three pelicans, a turtle, and dozens of fish.

"Bravo!" they cried.

Gull bowed. Seal smiled shyly. Buoy scanned the distant horizon.

"Encore!" the crowd demanded.

Buoy saw what he had hoped to see. He smiled too as Seal counted out the begining of their next song. Seal nodded toward him, and he rang his bell to the beat. Gull joined in. And as they played, Buoy watched the great tails of several Whales slap the surface three times each and then disappear joyfully beneath the waves.

隨著最後幾聲莊嚴的吠叫、尖叫與鈴鐺聲，
他們為演奏劃下了句點。

　　沈默。

　　然後是……潑濺的水聲、口哨，還有歡呼！

　　三位音樂家睜開眼睛，旁邊聚集著一群聽
眾。海豚、幾隻海獅、三隻塘鵝、一隻烏龜，加
上成群的魚。

　　「棒極了！」他們呼叫。

　　海鷗鞠躬，海豹帶著害羞的微笑，浮標則檢
視一下遠方的海平線。

　　「安可！」群眾要求。

　　浮標看到了他希望看到的情況。當海豹為下
一首歌倒數時，浮標也露出了微笑。海豹對著他
點點頭，浮標搖鈴應和著節拍，海鷗加了進來。
他們演奏時，浮標看到幾隻鯨魚的巨大尾巴分別
在水面上拍擊三下，然後歡悅地消失在海浪中。

storm

The night was always blackest during a storm, and a storm was always meanest at night. The Wind tore the Sea, picking up bits, flinging them about, and turning them into foam. The distant Clouds that had tumbled over each other at twilight now roared overhead, mostly invisible in the darkness, but adding their thunderous yell to the Wind's scream.

Buoy looked into the blackness and thought how harsh the world was during a storm. He was not frightened; he had seen many storms, and they did him no harm.

But he knew that storms could be dangerous to other creatures. And to ships.

暴風雨

　　暴風雨的夜晚總是最黑最暗的，而夜晚的暴風雨總是最兇最狠。風撕扯著海，捲起浪頭，恣意拋擲，將它們化為泡沫。會在薄暮時層層相疊的遠方雲朵，此刻在頂上呼嘯，大半消隱於黑暗中，以愈來愈強的雷鳴對抗著風的咆哮。

　　浮標凝視著黑暗，心想著，暴風雨中的世界是多麼粗暴啊。他並不害怕，他見過許多暴風雨，暴風雨不會傷害到他。

　　但是，他知道，暴風雨對別的生物很危險。對海上的船也是。

Buoy *enjoyed* the storm a little. The waves tried to drag him along as they roared past, but he stayed right where he was anchored. He would watch each wave as it rushed away toward the east, and then turn to face the next one as it approached, frothing with impatience.

Then he spotted the boat. It was a small boat, and Buoy knew immediately that something was wrong. Its sails were ripped and shredded. Out of control, it was being pushed sideways by the waves. A man and a woman and a tiny child huddled under the dodger as the fierce Wind tore at the remaining strips of canvas that hung from the mast. They did not see Buoy. Waves picked the boat up and hurled it wildly, nearly capsizing it. Buoy could tell there must already be a great deal of water in the boat because it floated low.

浮標有一點喜愛暴風雨。浪衝過來，努力要帶走浮標，可是，他硬是留在駐紮的地方。他會注視著每一道浪急湧向東方，再轉過頭去面對下一道浪，看著浪接近而來，帶著不耐吐出泡沫。

　　然後，他注意到一艘船。那是一艘小船，浮標一看就知道情況不對勁。船帆殘破不堪，航向失控，被海浪推著橫身漂盪。一個男人、一個女人，還有一個小孩一起擠在防浪屏下，暴風扯著桅桿上殘存的帆布條。他們沒有看見浮標。海浪把船舉高、猛烈地拋擲，幾乎把它倒翻過來。浮標看得出來，船上一定已經進了很多水，因為船身吃水很深。

As the boat came closer, Buoy gave his bell a mighty ring and flashed his light as brightly as he could. The woman looked up, grabbed the man´s arm, and pointed toward Buoy. Quickly the man made his way to the front of the boat, grabbed a line, and tied it to the bow. The little boat was moving fast. They would have only one chance.

　　船靠得更近時，浮標猛力搖鈴，盡力把光閃得極亮。那個女人抬頭，抓緊男人的手臂，伸手指向浮標。男人迅速走到船頭，抓起一條繩子，將它繫在船頭。小船的速度飛快，他們只有一次機會。

As the boat came close, Buoy leaned. He leaned with all the energy he had. With all of his will, he leaned toward the man´s outstretched hand. Buoy leaned until he could lean no farther. And just as he felt himself starting to roll back, the man´s fingers stretched an extra inch and grabbed Buoy´s mooring ring. The man quickly attached the rope and then returned to the stern where the woman was already bailing the water out.

When it looked as though they would not sink, the man and woman wrapped a blanket around their child and themselves. They stayed there all right, huddled on the floor of the boat, shivering against the cold Wind. Meanwhile, Buoy kept a watchful eye on them and tried as best he could to block the iciest of the storm´s blasts and the worst of the Sea´s waves.

當船靠近時，浮標傾斜，竭盡全力傾過去。他全心全意傾向那個男人伸出來的手，傾斜到不能再傾斜了。就在浮標覺得自己快要晃回來時，男人的手指又多延伸了一吋，緊緊抓住了浮標的碇泊圈。那男人迅速把纜索繫在上面，然後轉身走回船尾，而女人正在那裡將水舀出去。

　　當船看起來不會沉下去時，男人與女人用毯子將自己與小孩的身體包起來。他們整夜留在那裡，緊擁在甲板上，於冷風中發抖。同時，浮標小心翼翼地守望他們，盡可能阻擋冰冷的暴風雨和凶險的海浪。

In the morning the storm had blown itself away, and Buoy and the little boat bobbed on the Sea, which was still slightly upset from the night´s terror. The man, the woman, and the child unfolded themselves from their embrace and looked around, amazed that this sunny spot was the same one that had been so frightening only a few hours before.

Throughout the morning the man and the woman worked on the boat´s outboard motor. The child helped by finding misplaced tools and picking up lost screws. Gull, thinking the family might be hungry, dropped a small fish into the boat. Though they laughed, they didn´t eat it and instead threw it over the side. Seal swam about, playing peekaboo with the little one.

早晨，暴風雨走了，浮標和小船在海面上漂蕩。經過一夜的驚駭，海還有點不平靜。男人、女人與小孩從擁抱中解放開來，張望四周，不敢相信同樣的海面在幾個小時之前是那麼的恐怖，現在卻是陽光普照。

　　整個早晨，那男人與女人都在修理船的舷外馬達。小孩幫忙尋找放錯地方的工具，撿拾丟失的螺絲釘。海鷗想，這一家人恐怕肚子餓了，就把一條小魚丟到船裡。他們雖然笑了，卻把它丟到船邊，沒有吃它。海豹繞著船游來游去，和那小孩玩躲貓貓。

After many, many hours, with a groan and then a splutter, the motor came to life. The woman took the helm, and the man went to the bow. He carefully untied the line that had secured them through the long night. And, as he gently pushed the boat away, he whispered, "Thank you."

許多小時之後，隨著一聲呻吟聲和四濺的水花，馬達逐漸恢復了生命。女人過去掌舵，男人走向船頭，小心翼翼解開讓他們得以安全度過漫漫長夜的纜索。當他緩緩推船離去時，他輕輕說了一聲：「謝謝你。」

travelers

An egg carton, broken in half, floated by. It had been in the Sea for a very long time. Buoy could tell because it was worn and tired looking, and green sea grass hung from its bottom, delicately dancing in the currents.

"Hello, Buoy." Small voices came up from the carton. "Hello!"

Buoy looked down. "Hello, crabs," he said. "Where are you going?"

"To see the world Buoy. We're taking our ship and going to see the world."

"Wonderful," replied Buoy. "Do you know how to get there? Do you know which way to go?"

旅行家

　　一只裝蛋的紙盒子，破成兩截，漂了過來。它已經待在海上很久了，浮標看得出來，因為它傷痕累累，看來疲倦不堪，還有綠色的海草垂掛在底下，隨著水流優雅地舞動。

　　「哈囉，浮標，」紙盒裡有小小的聲音說：「哈囉！」

　　浮標往下看。「哈囉，螃蟹，」他說：「你們要去哪裡？」

　　「去看世界，浮標。我們乘著自己的船，要去看世界。」

　　「真好，」浮標答道：「你們知道怎麼去嗎？你們知道往哪裡走嗎？」

"Oh no! No, no,no!" cried the tiny crabs as they scurried over and under each other. "Do you?"

"I don´t," said Gull.

"Nor I," said Seal.

「哦，不知道！不知道！不知道！」這群小螃蟹大聲叫道，同時慌慌張張地互相爬上鑽下。「你們知道嗎？」

「我不知道。」海鷗說。

「我也不知道。」海豹說。

"Perhaps it´s across the Sea," Buoy suggested.

"The Sea? The Sea! Where is the Sea?" The crabs could barely keep themselves from falling over the edge of their egg carton as they clamored and crowded and crawled about.

Seal looked at Gull. Gull rolled his eyes, then flew away, groaning to himself.

Buoy thought for a moment. "Keep going," he said. "I think you´re heading in exactly the right direction."

The crabs scrambled to the front of their fragile ship. They peered over the edge, out across the never-ending blue.

"Ohhh," they whispered.

Their egg carton bobbed along, and Seal smiled.

Gull circled overhead, keeping an eye out for Shark. Buoy rang his bell gently and watched the travelers sail off in search of the world.

「大概要越過海洋。」浮標建議。

「海洋？海洋！海洋在哪裡？」螃蟹們吵吵鬧鬧，推來擠去，到處亂爬，差點就要掉到蛋盒子的外邊去了。

海豹看一下海鷗，海鷗轉了轉眼珠子，振翅飛走，自言自語地咕噥著。

浮標想了一會兒。「繼續前進，」他說：「我想，你們的方向完全正確。」

螃蟹攀爬到他們脆弱的船前面。他們從邊緣往下窺探，看見的是無邊無垠的藍。

「哦喔……」他們耳語著。

他們的蛋盒繼續漂蕩，海豹看了直笑。

海鷗在他們頭上盤旋，注意是不是有鯊魚出現。浮標輕輕搖鈴，注視著這群旅行家離開，去尋覓大千世界。

Voices, small and eager, floated back across the Wind. "Good-bye, Seal, good-bye, Gull, good-bye, Buoy."

"Good-bye, crabs," they replied. "Good luck."

Buoy rang his bell all night long that night, even though there was no storm and it was not foggy. Though the crabs were far away, he thought maybe they could still hear him through the damp blackness. He thought they would probably like that.

有聲音，小小的、急切的聲音，隨風飄回來。「再見，海豹！再見，海鷗！再見，浮標！」

　　「再見，螃蟹。」他們回答：「祝你們好運。」

　　那天晚上，浮標搖了整晚的鈴，雖然沒有風暴，也沒有起霧。儘管那群螃蟹已走遠了，他心中卻想著，也許鈴聲會穿越陰暗潮溼的夜，傳進他們的耳裡。說不定他們還挺喜歡的。

clouds

"It´s a herring," Gull said with authority. "What else could it be?"

"I think it looks like a crab," said Seal.

"You´re crazy," argued Gull."It´s a herring. And that one there is a fishing boat."

"No, it´s not. It´s a rock by the shore, perfect for sunning oneself on."

"Are you blind?" Gull asked."It´s a fishing boat! Don´t you see the nets? And the man tossing bait over the stern?"

"It´s a sunning rock," Seal insisted.

雲

「是鯡魚，」海鷗語帶權威：「要不然會是什麼東西？」

「我覺得它看起來像螃蟹。」海豹說。

「你發神經，」海鷗反駁道：「那是鯡魚，而那邊是漁船。」

「不，才不呢，那是海邊的一塊石頭，在上面曬太陽是最適合的。」

「你瞎眼了嗎？」海鷗問道：「那是一艘漁船！你沒有看見那些魚網嗎？還有那個正在船尾放餌的男人？」

「那是曬太陽用的石頭。」海豹頗堅持。

"You´ve been lying with your head too close to that bell!" Gull grumbled.

"What do you think, Buoy?" Seal asked.

Buoy looked up at the jumbly masses of white as they floated high in the pale blue Sky.

"I think they´re having fun," he said.

"Who?" Gull asked, quite annoyed. He wasn´t having fun.

"The Clouds," Buoy answered. "See how they roll around and pile on top of each other? They´re playing."

Gull flew off his perch and landed next to Seal. He looked up at Buoy and gave his wings an impatient flap.

"But who´s right? Is that a herring or a crab?" he demanded. "And is that one a fishing boat or a rock?"

「你一直躺在那邊，腦袋瓜離鈴鐺太近了！」海鷗咕噥說道。

「你認為呢？浮標。」海豹問。

浮標仰望那一片片高高飄浮在淡藍色天空中的亂雲。

「我想，他們正在玩耍。」浮標回答。

「誰？」海鷗問，他很不高興，他可不覺得好玩。

「雲啊，」浮標回答：「沒瞧見他們翻來滾去，都想爬到別人上面嗎？他們正在玩耍哩。」

海鷗飛離棲息點，在海豹身邊落下，他抬頭看著浮標，不耐地拍了一下翅膀。

「到底誰是對的？那到底是鯡魚還是螃蟹？」他質問道：「那是漁船還是石頭？」

Buoy stared at the great billowing Clouds.
Gull paced. Seal laid her head back down and
closed her eyes. Finally Buoy spoke.

"Well, Gull, that one looks like you. And the
other one looks like Seal."

　　浮標瞪著奔湧的大片雲團。海鷗踱來踱去。
海豹又低下頭來，閉上眼睛。終於，浮標說話
了。

　　「這個嘛，海鷗，那個看起來像你，而另一
個，看起來像海豹。」

"Ohhh!" Gull flew up to his perch and turned his back on the Clouds. "Why do I bother!"

"What´s the matter? What did I say?" Buoy asked, surprised.

"Nothing, Buoy." Seal said without raising her head. She smiled. "Just the truth, that's all."

「哈！」海鷗飛回他棲息的位置，背對著雲，「我才不在乎呢！」

「怎麼一回事？我說了什麼？」浮標問道，顯得很驚訝。

「沒事，浮標，」海豹說，頭都沒抬一下。她微笑。「就是事實而已。」

slick

It was interesting to see, but it felt wrong. A yellow glow to the north. It wasn´t the Moon. And it wasn´t ships´ lights. It wasn´t Stars either, though Seal suggested that maybe a Star had fallen a little way away. Buoy didn´t think so. Whatever it was, it lit up the night sky and changed it to an uncomfortable orange, sometimes flickering green and then blue or red or white.

"I don´t like it," said Gull.

Neither did Buoy.

The next morning Buoy felt sticky. He felt sluggish and slow. He opened his eyes and looked around. The Sun was just beginning to light up the Sea. But where was the blue?

光滑

　　看起來有趣，但又覺得怪怪的。北方有黃光閃耀，不是月亮，也不是船的燈光。那不是星星，雖然海豹表示那可能是一顆流星，可是浮標並不這麼想。不管是什麼，它照亮了夜空，把天空變成了令人不舒服的橘子色，有時會閃成綠色，然後是藍色、紅色或白色。

　　「我不喜歡它。」海鷗說。

　　浮標也不喜歡。

　　第二天早晨，浮標覺得身體黏黏的。他覺得自己變得呆滯緩慢，他張開雙目看看四周。太陽剛剛要開始照亮海面，但藍色到哪裡去了？

As far as Buoy could see, the Sea was black. Shining black and gray. Buoy could feel the blackness cling to him as he rolled with the low swell. The black even seemed to be trying to stop the swell. It seemed to be trying to smother anything that wasn´t black.

"Gull! Seal! Wake up!" Buoy called.

"What´s the mat—Oh!" said Seal.

"Will you keep the racket down," grouched Gull."It's too early for all this yell—Oh...Oh! Oil!"

"What?" asked Buoy."What is it?"

"Oil," echoed Seal. "It´s oil, Buoy."

"That´s what we saw last night," said Gull. "A ship must have caught fire and spilled all this."

浮標看得見的海面都是黑漆漆的，閃著黑與灰的光澤。隨著低低的波潮流動時，浮標感覺得到黑暗糾纏著他。那黑色似乎還要阻止潮湧，企圖悶死任何不是黑色的東西。

「海鷗！海豹！醒來！」浮標叫喊道。

「什麼事……啊……」海豹說。

「不要那麼吵好嗎？」海鷗抱怨：「一大早就大喊大叫……啊……油！」

「什麼？」浮標問：「那是什麼？」

「油。」海豹重覆：「是油，浮標。」

「那就是我們昨天晚上看到的，」海鷗說。「一定是有一艘船著火了，洩出這些油來。」

They sat in silence for a while and looked across the sad blackness toward the place where they had seen the strange light the night before.

"Seal," Gull said suddenly, "we have to go."

"I know," she said.

"What?" cried Buoy. "You can´t leave me here in the middle of all this...oil!"

"We have to, Buoy," said Seal. "We´re sorry, but we must. Gull can´t fish through the oil. If it gets on him he won´t be able to fly. And I can only swim in it for so long. It´s poison."

"Will you come back?" Buoy asked softly.

"Of course we will. As soon as it´s safe."

And then they left, Seal swimming underwater for as long as she could and Gull slowly circling above her to make sure she was all right.

他們靜靜坐了一會兒，視線穿過那令人悲傷的黑色地帶，朝向昨晚閃著奇怪亮光的地方。

　　「海豹，」海鷗突然說：「我們必須走了。」

　　「我知道。」她說。

　　「什麼？」浮標喊道：「你們不能把我留在這些……油裡面！」

　　「浮標，我們必須離開。」海豹說。「我們很抱歉，可是，我們一定得走。海鷗不能在油水裡覓食，他要是沾上油，就不能飛了，而我待在油水中的時間也夠久了，油有毒。」

　　「你們會回來嗎？」浮標輕聲問著。

　　「我們當然會回來，只要安全了就回來。」

　　說完，他們就動身離去，海豹潛入水底盡量走遠，海鷗在她的上空盤旋，確定她一切安好。

Buoy watched them go. Straining to see Seal´s head pop up through the murky goo, he shuddered to think of the blackness actually touching his friend.

　　浮標看著他們離去，緊張地看著海豹的頭頂從骯髒的黏物中掙出頭來。想到那黑黑的油垢確實沾附在他朋友的身上，他就會發抖。

When he could see them no longer he turned and looked around. He noticed a thin wisp of smoke rising in the north. He was very sad. He felt sorry for himself because he was alone. He felt sorry for Gull and Seal because they had to leave their home. But mostly, as he looked out over the thick black ooze, he felt sorry for the Sea. Because the Sea had nowhere to go.

當他們消失不見時，他轉了轉，看看周遭。他注意到一小縷煙由北方冒起。他很悲傷，為自己感到難過，因為他孤零零的。他也為海鷗與海豹難過，因為他們必須離開自己的家。然而，看著眼前濃稠的黑漬，他最感到難過的是海，因為海無處可走。

birthday

Many days passed, and Seal and Gull finally returned. As did the blue of the Sea.

Buoy awoke one morning to feel something tugging on him.

"Seal! Gull! Wake up! Something's got me!"

Seal looked up sleepily. "Hmmm?"

Gull flapped his wings twice in irritation. "Keep quiet, Buoy. It's early."

"No, no!" cried Buoy. "Something's got me!"

Gull and Seal opened their eyes again, looked around, and smiled.

生 日

　　過了許多天，海鷗與海豹終於回來了，而海也重新變藍了。

　　有一天早晨，浮標醒來，覺得有東西在拉他。

　　「海豹！海鷗！醒來！有東西在拉我！」

　　海豹抬頭，睡眼惺忪。「唔？」

　　海鷗不耐地拍了兩次翅膀。「安靜，浮標，才一大早呢。」

　　「不行，不行！」浮標喊道：「有東西在拉我。」

　　海鷗與海豹再度睜開眼，看了看四周，笑了起來。

"Don´t worry, Buoy." Seal laughed. "I think *you´ve* got it."

"What?" cried Buoy, still very nervous. "What have I got?"

Gull grabbed the something and pulled it away from Buoy´s light, where it had tangled itself during the night. He flew down next to Seal with the thing flying from his beak.

Buoy looked at it. Awe filled his heart. It was so beautiful! Red, just as he was. With a white ribbon curling gracefully below. And it flew— bobbing and bouncing in the air, just as he bobbed and bounced on the Sea,

"What is it?" Buoy asked, almost breathless with wonder.

「別擔心，浮標，」海豹笑出聲：「我看你中獎了。」

「什麼？」浮標喊道，還是很緊張：「我中了什麼？」

海鷗抓起那東西，把它從浮標的燈上拉開，也就是它昨晚纏上去的地方。海鷗飛下來，停在海豹身邊，那東西在他的喙上飛舞著。

浮標看著那東西，心中充滿敬畏。它好美麗，是紅色的，就像以前的浮標，它底下還繫著一條白色絲帶，曲線優雅。它在風中蹦蹦跳跳的，就像他自己在海上蹦蹦跳跳一樣。

「那是什麼？」浮標問，驚奇到幾乎無法呼吸。

Gull held the ribbon with his feet so he could speak. "It´s a ballon, Buoy."

"There´s writing on it, Gull," said Seal. "What does it say?"

Gull looked hard at the balloon, and he thought hard too. "It says 'Hap...py Bir...th...day. Happy Birthday!' "

"*Thank you!*" Buoy practically exploded. Gull, surprised, jumped back and almost lost his hold on the balloon. "You remembered my birthday!" exclaimed Buoy. "What wonderful friends you are. I didn´t even know it was my birthday!"

"But Buoy," Seal began, "it wasn´t—"

"Hrmph!" Gull shushed Seal. "We´re glad you like it," he said to Buoy.

海鷗用腳抓住彩帶，以便開口說話：「是一個氣球，浮標。」

　　「上面有字，海鷗，」海豹說。「寫什麼？」

　　海鷗努力看著氣球，也努力在想。「上面寫著『生…日…快…樂，生日快樂』！」

　　「謝謝你們！」浮標樂翻了。海鷗被他嚇得往後跳，差點抓不住氣球。「你們記得我的生日！」浮標嘆道：「你們真是我的好朋友，我都不知道自己的生日呢！」

　　「可是，浮標，」海豹開口說：「那不是……」

　　「噓！」海鷗阻止海豹。「我們真高興你喜歡這個禮物。」他對浮標說。

"I do. Yes, I do," said Buoy. "Please, Gull, put it back on my light for me."

Gull flew up and carefully tied the balloon to Buoy´s light. And there it stayed for many, many days.

「我喜歡，哇，我喜歡，」浮標說。「拜託你，海鷗，請你把它放回我的燈上。」

海鷗飛起來，小心地將氣球繫在浮標的燈上，汽球就在那裡待了很多天。

new paint

Men came in a big boat and pulled Buoy up out of the water with a crane.

Gull flew off, complaining with loud screeches. No one took notice. Seal floated a little bit away, wondering what was going on.

The men looked at Buoy very carefully. They looked at his light and at his bell. They scraped off the long sea grass that hung from his bottom. They rubbed him with rough brushes wherever he was rusty, and they replaced one of the wires that ran to his light. Then they painted him. Red. Bright, glossy red.

A brighter red than Buoy could ever remember being. And when he was dry, they gently lowered him back into the Sea.

新漆

　　男人們坐著大船過來，用起重機把浮標從水中拉起。

　　海鷗飛離那裡，以響亮的尖聲咆嘯抱怨，但沒有人注意。海豹稍微漂離那裡，不明白是怎麼一回事。

　　男人們很仔細地檢查浮標。他們檢查他的燈和鈴鐺。他們刮除掛在他底下的長長海草，用粗刷子把鏽刷掉，還換了一條燈線，然後為他塗漆。是紅的，亮麗、光鮮的紅。

　　浮標不記得自己曾經這麼鮮紅過。等他乾了，他們就輕輕將他放回海裡。

When the men left, Seal jumped up and settled back into her accustomed place. She sniffed once at the new paint and then laid her head down and closed her eyes.

　　那些男人離開之後，海豹跳上去，在她習慣的位置上安頓下來。她嗅一嗅新漆，把頭靠上去，閉上眼睛。

Gull flew down and landed on his perch on Buoy´s head. His feet slipped a little on the slick finish, and he cast his eyes critically over Buoy.

"You´re different," said Gull.

"Not really," said Buoy. "I just look different."

"Hmmm," said Gull thoughtfully. "All right then."

海鷗飛下來，在他位於浮標頭上的棲息點降落，他的腳在滑溜的新漆上稍微滑了一下，然後把浮標仔細端詳一番。

　　「你不一樣了。」海鷗說。

　　「也沒有啦。」浮標說：「我只是看起來不一樣。」

　　「嗯……」海鷗慎重地說：「這樣也好。」

pup

"Seal, you´re getting fat," said Buoy.

Gull snickered. Seal smiled.

"I´m not getting fat," said Seal.

"Well...plump then," said Buoy, trying to be polite. "You´re getting a little bit plump."

Gull guffawed. Seal smiled again.

"That´s not what I meant," she said.

"Well, what did you mean?" asked Buoy, a bit irritated at Gull´s laugh.

Gull couldn´t stand it any longer.

"She´s not fat, you bell-brain, she´s pregnant!"

"Pregnant? Wow," said Buoy. "You mean you´re going to have a pup?"

小 海 豹

「海豹，你胖了。」浮標說。

海鷗竊喜，海豹微笑。

「我不是長胖。」海豹說。

「那……就說是發福好了。」浮標說，他想要表現禮貌。「你是有一點發福了。」

海鷗大笑，海豹又微微一笑。

「我不是這個意思。」她說。

「那，你是什麼意思？」浮標問。海鷗的笑聲使他有一點惱怒。

海鷗再也忍不住了。

「她不是胖了，你這鈴鐺腦袋，她懷孕了。」

「懷孕？哇！」浮標說：「妳的意思是，妳要生小海豹了？」

"Yes," said Seal. And she smiled a third time.

Many days passed, and then one morning Seal swam away toward the east.

More days passed. And more. Far too many for Buoy. He was lonely without Seal.

Gull would fly east every so often and bring back reports.

"Any day now."

"It´ll be soon."

"Tomorrow. Count on it."

"I feel it in my feathers. Tomorrow for sure."

"Yep, tomorrow is the day. As sure as there´s fish in the Sea."

And finally...

"It´s a girl!"

「是的。」海豹說，第三次微笑。

許多天過去了，有一天早晨，海豹動身游向東方。

很多天過去了，更多天過去了。對浮標來說，太多天了。沒有海豹，他覺得寂寞。

海鷗常常飛向東方，帶回一些消息。

「隨時會生了。」

「快了。」

「明天，相信我！」

「我的每一根羽毛都覺得，明天一定會生。」

「一定的，就是明天了，就像海水中一定有魚一般，錯不了。」

終於……

「是個女孩！」

More days passed. Buoy couldn´t stand it!

"When are they coming?" he´d cry, and then he´d beg Gull to fly east and check on them just one more time.

At last Seal came back. With her she had her newborn pup, short and round and big-eyed and wondering.

這麼多天過去了，浮標再也等不及了！

「他們什麼時候回來？」他大喊，然後邀求海鷗飛去東邊，再次弄清楚。

最後，海豹回來了。帶著她新生的小海豹，短短、圓圓的，大眼睛充滿驚奇。

"Daughter," Seal said, "this is Buoy."

"Hello, Buoy. Hello."

"Nice to meet you," said Buoy.

"Yes, it is," said the pup. Then she looked at him closely.

"Who are you?" she asked.

"I´m Buoy," Buoy answered.

"What´s a *buoy*?" asked the pup.

"Well," said Buoy, "I´m someone to climb on for rest. I´ll protect you from Shark. And I´m someone to talk to and look at the Moon with. And I´m here all the time. And I´ll tell you about ships and how I keep them safe with my light. And about the Green Flash and the Whales' song. And we can watch Falling Stars together. And talk to Porpoise. I´ll ring my bell for you. And I´ll rock you to sleep every night."

The pup looked up at Seal, wondering what Buoy was talking about.

「女兒，」海豹說：「這是浮標。」

「哈囉，浮標。哈囉！

「真高興見到妳。」浮標說。

「是的。」小海豹說，然後仔細看著浮標。

「你是誰？」她問。

「我是浮標。」浮標回答。

「什麼是浮標？」小海豹問。

「這個嘛，」浮標說：「我是可以讓妳爬上來休息的東西，我會保護妳不被鯊魚傷害，我會和妳談天，一起看月亮，我永遠都在這邊。我會說船的故事給妳聽，我會告訴你我是怎麼用閃光去保護船，告訴妳綠光和鯨魚之歌的故事。我們可以一同看流星，和海豚說話。我會為妳響鈴，每天晚上搖你入睡。」

小海豹仰起頭看看媽媽，不明白浮標在說什麼。

Seal jumped up onto Buoy. "He´s one of the family," she said. "This is our home."

Buoy beamed. He looked at the new pup splashing at his side. At Seal lying on her back, leaning warmly against him.

At Gull flying overhead, keeping an eye out for Shark. At the white Clouds playing charades in the blue Sky. He looked at the Sea. Her long low swells approaching so gracefully, so smoothly. A constant greeting he knew so well. The Sea in which he lived. In which they all lived.

Yes, he thought, *this is home.*

海豹跳到浮標上面。「他是我們的家人。」她說：「這是我們的家。」

　　浮標閃起亮光。他望著在他身邊玩水的小海豹，望著海豹仰臥在他上面，溫暖地倚靠著他。

　　他看看海鷗，海鷗在頭上面飛，提防鯊魚來襲。他看看白雲，白雲正在藍天玩排字遊戲。他看看海，舒緩低平的海潮接近而來，如此優雅，如此靜謐，頻頻捎來他所熟知的問候。他住在海裡，他們都住在海裡。

　　是的，浮標想，這就是家。

關於作者

布魯斯貝倫　BRUCE BALAN

　　一名悠游海洋的水手與潛水專家。在一次夜航中，貝倫與叔叔保羅在加州佛明岬角附近初遇浮標！

　　近年來，布魯斯貝倫投入寫作，成為一名全職作家。已出版的作品包括幾本發人省思的繪本及一套神秘系列作品，他目前與妻子黛娜定居加州。

■ 關於繪者

洛爾科隆　RAÚL COLÓN

　　一位值得喝采的當代插畫家。科隆的作品散見於無數書本封面、雜誌及報紙等，並贏得多次「插畫家協會」、「紐約時報最佳繪本書」等年度大獎。

　　洛爾科隆為道地紐約客，自小於現代藝術之都耳濡目染之外，並赴波多黎各學習商業藝術，之後將自己的黃金十年貢獻給位於佛羅里達的教育電台，另外亦從事動畫、布偶及佈景設計工作。

愛藏本 26　浮　標

文字	布魯斯貝倫
插畫	洛爾科隆
譯者	晨星編譯組
文字編輯	張惠凌
美術編輯	柳惠芬

發行人	陳銘民
發行所	晨星出版社
	台中市工業區30路1號
	TEL:(04)3595820　　FAX:(04)3595493
	E-mail　morning @tcts.seed.net.tw
	郵政劃撥：02319825
	行政院新聞局局版台業字第2500號
法律顧問	甘龍強律師
製作印刷	知文企業（股）公司　　　(04)23595819-120
初版	中華民國88年 2月28日
再版	中華民國92年10月31日

總經銷	知己實業股份有限公司
	〈台北公司〉台北市羅斯福路二段 79 號 4F 之 9
	TEL:(02)23672044　FAX:(02)23635741
	〈台中公司〉台中市工業區 30 路 1 號
	TEL:(04)23595819　FAX:(04)23595493

定價160元　　　ISBN 957-455-531-3

國家圖書館出版品預行編目資料

浮標：家在海上／布魯斯貝倫文字；洛爾科隆
插畫；晨星編譯組翻譯.－－再版.－－臺中市：
晨星.2003〔民92〕
　　　面；　公分.－－（愛藏本；26）
　　　譯自；Buoy: home at sea
　　　　ISBN 957-455-531-3(平裝)

874.57　　　　　　　　　　　92015927

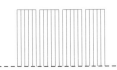
更方便的購書方式：

(1)**信用卡訂閱**　填妥「信用卡訂購單」，傳真至本公司。
　　　　　　　或　填妥「信用卡訂購單」，郵寄至本公司。

(2)**郵政劃撥**　帳戶：晨星出版有限公司　帳號：22326758
　　　　　　　在通信欄中填明叢書編號、書名、定價及總金
　　　　　　　額即可。

(3)**通　　信**　填妥訂購人資料，連同支票寄回。

◉如需更詳細的書目，可來電或來函索取。
◉購買單本以上9折優待，5本以上85折優待，10本以上8折優待。
◉訂購3本以下如需掛號請另付掛號費30元。
◉服務專線：(04)23595819-231　FAX：(04)23597123
　E-mail:itmt@ms55.hinet.net

◆讀者回函卡◆

讀者資料：

姓名：_____ 性別：□ 男 □ 女

生日： ／ ／ 身分證字號：_____

地址：□□□_____

聯絡電話： （公司） （家中）

E-mail _____

職業：□ 學生 □ 教師 □ 內勤職員 □ 家庭主婦
　　　□ SOHO族 □ 企業主管 □ 服務業 □ 製造業
　　　□ 醫藥護理 □ 軍警 □ 資訊業 □ 銷售業務
　　　□ 其他_____

購買書名：_____

您從哪裡得知本書：□ 書店 □ 報紙廣告 □ 雜誌廣告 □ 親友介紹
□ 海報 □ 廣播 □ 其他：_____

您對本書評價： （請填代號 1. 非常滿意 2. 滿意 3. 尚可 4. 再改進）

封面設計_____版面編排_____內容_____文／譯筆_____

您的閱讀嗜好：

□ 哲學 □ 心理學 □ 宗教 □ 自然生態 □ 流行趨勢 □ 醫療保健
□ 財經企管 □ 史地 □ 傳記 □ 文學 □ 散文 □ 原住民
□ 小說 □ 親子叢書 □ 休閒旅遊 □ 其他_____

信用卡訂購單 （要購書的讀者請填以下資料）

書　　　　名	數　量	金　額	書　　　　名	數　量	金　額

□VISA　□JCB　□萬事達卡　□運通卡　□聯合信用卡

- 卡號：_____ ●信用卡有效期限：_____年_____月

- 訂購總金額：_____元 ●身分證字號：_____

- 持卡人簽名：_____ （與信用卡簽名同）

- 訂購日期：_____年_____月_____日

填妥本單請直接郵寄回本社或傳真(04)23597123